SCHOOL SIDEKICKS
FIELD DAY FUN

by Molly Beth Griffin

illustrated by Mike Deas

PICTURE WINDOW BOOKS
a capstone imprint

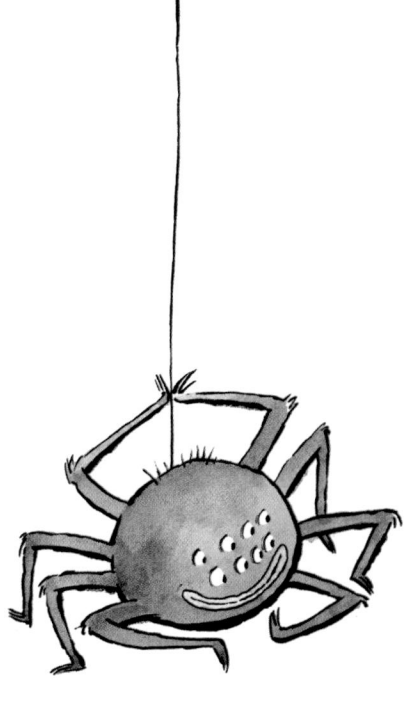

TABLE OF CONTENTS

SCHOOL SIDEKICKS

These five friends live within the walls, nooks, and crannies of an elementary school. They learn alongside kids every day, even though the kids don't see them!

STELLA

Stella is a mouse. She loves her friends. She also loves children and school! She came into the school on a cold winter day. She knew it would be her home forever. Her favorite subjects are social studies and music. She is always excited for a new day.

BO

Bo is a parakeet. He is a classroom pet. The friends let him out of his cage so they can play together. Bo loves to read. He goes home with his teacher on weekends, but he always comes back to school to see his friends.

DELILAH

Delilah is a spider. She has always lived in the corners of the school. She is so small the children never notice her, but she is very smart. Delilah loves math and computers and hates the broom.

NICO

Nico is a toad. He used to be a classroom pet. A child forgot to put him back into his tank one day. Now he lives with his friends. The whole school is his home! He can be grumpy, but he loves science and art. Since Nico doesn't have fingers, he paints with his toes!

GOLDIE

Goldie is a goldfish. She is very wise. The friends ask her questions when they have a big choice to make. She gives good advice and lives in the media center.

SUN AND FUN

When Stella the Mouse woke up, light poured in through the windows. The sun was out. The sky was blue.

"Hurray!" she cried.

She woke up Nico the Toad, Delilah the Spider, and Bo the Parakeet.

"Perfect weather for a fun field day!" she cried.

The friends had decided to brave going outside for this special day. Now it was here!

All the children were having fun. They were running, playing, and shouting, so nobody noticed four small animals.

The animals stretched. They jogged in place to warm up. They worked on their cheer.

"One, two, three, four! Hear us roar! See us soar! Five, six, seven, eight! We can't wait! Make it great!"

Nico joined in the long jump.

He was a good jumper.

Delilah lined up
for the three-legged
race. She had
plenty of legs.

Stella wanted to run the relay.

"We'll work together as a
team!" she squeaked.

"I'm in," said Nico.

"Me too," said Delilah.

"Great," said Stella. "Bo?"

"No way," said Bo, and he flew away.

They found him under a tree, reading his book.

"Come on, Bo!" said Nico.

"We need four to make a team," said Delilah.

"It will be fun," said Stella.

He shook his head and buried his beak in the book.

"What do we do?" Stella asked Nico and Delilah.

"Let's go ask Goldie," said Nico.

The friends often went to see Goldie when they had a big question or needed advice.

She was a wise goldfish. She
lived in the media center.

"Good plan," said Delilah.

They left Bo to read under his
tree. They scurried and hopped
and crept off to find Goldie.

Chapter 2

THE PROBLEM

"Goldie! We want to run the relay, but Bo won't join our team," Stella said.

"Can we do it without him?" asked Nico.

Goldie swam in a circle.

"Blub, blub," she said.

One blub meant yes. Two blubs meant no. At least that's what the friends thought she meant.

"You're right," said Delilah. "The teams have to have four. That's the rule! Without him, we are just three."

"And he looks so sad and lonely," said Stella.

"So how do we get him to join us?" Nico asked.

Goldie just stared at them. Usually she had answers. Today she just seemed to be shrugging her fins. She seemed to be asking them why.

"Maybe we should ask him why he doesn't want to join in?" said Stella. "If we can figure that out, maybe we can solve the problem."

"Blub," said Goldie.

The friends scurried and hopped and crept back outside.

"Bo!" squeaked Stella. "Why don't you want to run the relay?"

Bo looked up from his book.

"If I tell you, you'll laugh at me," he said.

"We won't," said Nico.

"We promise," said Delilah.

Stella sat down beside him and put her paw on his wing.

"Because I can't run," Bo mumbled.

Stella started to laugh. Bo
looked angry.

"I'm not laughing at you,
Bo. I'm laughing at ALL of us.
Because none of us can run!"
Stella said.

Bo looked confused.

"I don't really run," said Stella.

"I scurry and scamper. See?"

She showed him.

"And I don't run either. I hop and leap," said Nico. "See?"

"I creep and crawl," said Delilah. "See?"

"We all move differently," said Stella. "And that's great!"

Bo smiled.

"I flap and flutter," he said. "And I can hop a little too. Just like you, Nico."

"Perfect!" said Stella. "Let's race!"

THE RACE

The friends found a twig to use as their baton. They lined up at the starting line. They yelled their cheer together.

"One, two, three, four! Hear us roar! See us soar! Five, six, seven, eight! We can't wait! Make it great!"

The whistle blew.

Stella scurried. Then she passed
the twig to Nico.

Nico hopped. He passed the twig to Delilah.

Delilah crept. Then she passed the twig to Bo.

"Go, Bo, go!" they all cried.

He didn't just fly. He soared!

The friends were fast, but the children had long legs. They were much faster. The friends lost by a mile.

But it didn't feel that way.

It felt good to move in the warm, bright sunshine. It felt good to be a team and have fun together. It felt good to be brave and go outside.

Stella's wish for a fabulous field day had really come true!

TALK ABOUT IT

1. Going outside was scary for the animal friends. Talk about something that scares you. How can you conquer your fear?

2. Field day is fun, but it can make some people feel left out. How can you make everyone feel included?

3. Did you know why Bo didn't want to join the relay race? Were there any clues in the story?

WRITE ABOUT IT

1. Make a list of three field day events you would like to try. Next to each event, write what you can do to practice.

2. Pretend you are one of the animal friends. Write a journal entry about field day.

3. Write a letter of encouragement to the animal friends for field day.

MOLLY BETH GRIFFIN

Molly Beth Griffin is a writing teacher at the Loft Literary Center in Minneapolis, Minnesota. She has written numerous picture books (including *Loon Baby* and *Rhoda's Rock Hunt*) and a YA novel *(Silhouette of a Sparrow)*. Molly loves reading and hiking in all kinds of weather. She lives in South Minneapolis with her partner and two kids.

MIKE DEAS

Mike Deas is a cartoonist, illustrator, and graphic novelist. His love for illustrative storytelling comes from an early love of reading and drawing. Capilano College's Commercial Animation Program in Vancouver helped Mike fine-tune his drawing skills and imagination. Mike lives with his family on sunny Salt Spring Island, British Columbia, Canada.

PLENTY OF SIDEKICK FUN!

School Sidekicks is published by
Picture Window Books, a Capstone Imprint
1710 Roe Crest Drive, North Mankato, Minnesota 56003
www.capstonepub.com

Library of Congress Cataloging-in-Publication Data
can be found on the Library of Congress database

ISBN: 978-1-5158-4418-1 (library binding)
ISBN: 978-1-5158-4422-8 (eBook pdf)

Summary: Field day arrives, and Stella the Mouse, Nico the Toad, Delilah
the Spider, and Bo the Parakeet are excited to join in the fun. Stella wants
everyone to be a team for the relays. But Bo says no. He just wants to sit
under a tree with his book. Can they be a team without him?

Designer: Ted Williams

Design elements: Shutterstock: AVA Bitter, design element throughout,
Oleksandr Rybitskiy, design element throughout

Printed and bound in the United States of America.
PA71